Ready to Glow

Adapted by P. J. Rudi • Designed by Sophia Yoon

No part of this work may be reproduced in whole or in part, or stored in a retrieval system, or transmitted in any form or by any means, electronic, mechanical, photocopying, recording, or otherwise, without written permission of the publisher. For information regarding permission, write to Scholastic Inc., Attention: Permissions Department, 557 Broadway, New York, NY 10012.

ISBN 0-439-73386-3

TROLLZ TM & © 2005 DIC ENTERTAINMENT. Under License from DAM
All rights reserved. Published by Scholastic Inc.
SCHOLASTIC and associated logos are trademarks and/or registered trademarks of Scholastic Inc.

12 11 10 9 8 7 6 5 4 3 2 1   5 6 7 8 9/0

Printed in the U.S.A.
First printing, October 2005

SCHOLASTIC INC.
New York   Toronto   London   Auckland   Sydney
Mexico City   New Delhi   Hong Kong   Buenos Aires

I'm late!
My friends are waiting!

Yeah!

Nothing gets between me . . . my
friends . . . and, of course, the mall.

They're here! Just like always!

So I'm like, "You mess with my friends, you mess with me."

You go, troll!

Hi! I'm back from vacation!

It's so true. Friends are even more important than hair gel!

Hello? It's me, Amethyst!

Don't you remember?
I was away all summer!

It's time for our
Re-do the 'do *Party!*

Topaz! Ruby!
Onyx! Sapphire!

Can't you see me?
Don't you know me?!

AAAAAA...AAH!!

It was just a dream.

Amethyst? Are you okay?

I just had the worst nightmare.

I went to the mall and my friends didn't know me. It's like I wasn't there.

You haven't changed that much in one summer.

And even if you did, friendships evolve, and good friends adjust.

Relax. There's *no way* they'll be late.

Time for a troll stroll!

Over here!

I missed you guys so much.

Amethyst!

8

Ruby!

Watch the hair.

**Squeal with delight
and I'll puke.**

9

I had this weird dream that I wouldn't fit in with you guys anymore.

Am, that's crazy.

Nobody busts up the crew.

How can we be Best Friends For Life if we're not friends, like, *now*?

Cute boy at three o'clock.

But it's only ten-thirty.

Over there!

Hottie!

Stylish.

Lost soul.

Cool sneaks.

Um... I think he looks like he might be nice and fun to study with?

Somebody is *seriously* out of practice.

Sorry, guys. I've had a lot on my mind lately.

Why?

It's kind of a secret.

Spill!

Well... okay. I *did* want to tell you guys.

My gem got its glow!

Awesome!

It's about time you joined the rest of us. Show us a spell.

My grandmother told me not to waste spells. They're expensive!

Here! I've got tons of them.

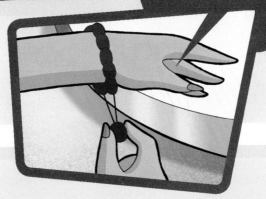

Oh, cool! We both got transformation spells!

Oooohhh!

She could use some help.

Drab and dreary, walking by,
Look pretty as a butterfly.

Oh!

A new hairdo would have been fine. This could get us in major trouble.

Cut me some slack. You've gotta admit she looks better.

Real nice 'tude, Ruby.

Hey, rookie.
We need help here.

I can't.

You've got to, Amethyst.

Trapped in a body not your own,
Release your spirit to the shape
you've known.

Awesome!

Am, you're a natural at this magic stuff.

We could have a new spell champ.

Or we *could* have beginner's luck.

I guess I should go where my magic's appreciated.

Let's go, Topaz. Our turn to calm down the drama queen.

Onyx, what did I do?

Nothing. Ruby gets jealous. It'll be fine.

Sadly, I'm late for my dentist and his dark room of pain. Later.

But she was so mad.

Ohmigosh! My nightmare's coming true!

I don't fit in with my friends anymore!

I don't know why Mom says I'm unorganized.

My photo album! Right where I left it.

Hey, Wa-wa!

Memory book on.

Gonna have to
update that photo.

Let's see.
Favorite memories.

Eight years old.
Camp out!

Let's play Girl
Power Tower.

Okay!

Amethyst... you and Onyx on the bottom.

Okay!

How come we always get the bottom?

Mystic Waterfall!

That's better.

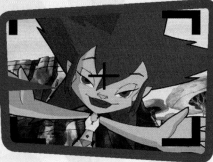

Everybody ready?

Wait a sec. Amethyst, we need you to hold the camera.

Okay.

Girl power!

Memory book off.

Now I get why I don't fit in anymore.

I never used to do anything but follow them around and do what they wanted.

I *can't* be that way anymore.

Can I?

You want to do what?

I want to try to be like I used to be.

And I thought you'd stepped it up... becoming all grown up and cool.

You did?

Yeah. I'll bet Topaz and Sapphire think so, too.

You're older now. You're going to be better at some things than Ruby is.

But I don't want her mad at me. What do I do?

I'd just let it go. But knowing you . . . you'll want to get all mushy.

Hey, kid! You gonna order something or just sit there like a bump on a log?

Bump on a log... knot on the bark... howl like a dog... hunt like the snark!

Now THAT'S sweet.

Um, hi, Flint. Have you seen Ruby today?

I've been so deep in my own head today I have not even seen, like, the sun.

Oh. Well... thanks.

Hey, Amethyst!

Yes?

I'm a bump on a log.

Hey, Flint!

Guess who just bench-pressed 320?

40

Personal best!

Hey, kid! Pick those up.

Whoa! We should know each other.

We do, Rock. I'm Amethyst.

Whoa! I already know a girl named Amethyst.

Yeah. It's me.

Whoa! Coincidence!

42

What?

First she tries to wreck the crew, and now she's putting moves on *my* boyfriend.

Are you and Rock going out?

Duh! I just haven't told him yet.

Ruby! Am I glad to see you!

Yeah, I'll bet. Traitor!

No, this is Amethyst.

I'm sorry about before. I just want to be in the crew again.

So that's why you steal my boyfriend?

Your boyfriend? Who's that?!

You!

What?

Ruby, I didn't steal your—

As far as I'm concerned, you're out of the crew! Forever!

WHAT?!

Whoa. Harsh.

You're taking her side?! That's it! We're through!

Did we just break up?

You'll still have your memories.

Memories of what?

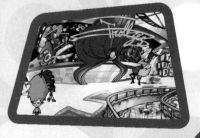

The middle dryer has the best boy-viewing in the mall.

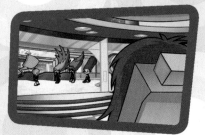

You can dry your hair and watch boys at the same time? Wow.

Cute senior straight ahead.

Amethyst, look! He's perfect for...

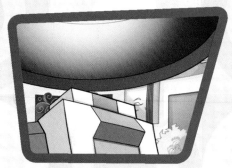

That's where she always sits. It makes sense that you miss her.

Who says I miss her?

Um... I just did.

So, let me get this straight....

You know Amethyst wants to be back in the crew.

Right.

And you know that Ruby wants Amethyst back in the crew.

Right.

Yet we all know it will never happen, because Ruby is too proud to admit she was wrong.

Well, duh.

No, Saph. It means we have to do something special. . . .

Which means... we can't fix it and we all have to stop being friends?

Something risky...

You're not thinking...

You don't mean...

Magic!

Uh... hi, Am. I was just skooting through your neighborhood. Thought I'd say hi.

No! I can't apologize.

be-eep!

Hello?

Hey, Ruby!

Hey, Tope! What's up?

Nothing special... Oh, right! Onyx and Sapphire found out about a party at the old clearing...

... where we used to have sleepovers.

A party?!

I'm there!

53

Hi, Tope.

What about Ruby?

She, uh... wants to say she's sorry... you know, about kicking you out and everything.

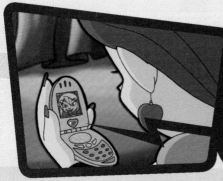

She does?!

She's just too embarrassed to ask you herself.

She said she'll meet you at the old clearing where we used to have pajama parties.

Tell her I'm on my way!

Ruby?

I look good.

Now!

Sprig of fir and leaf of clover, Turn our Topaz into an ogre.

Ungh... Uh...

Oh...

Umm... Ow

What do you think?

Awesome.

Now let's go scare them back together.

Amethyst?!

Ruby! They said you'd come.

Who said I'd come?

Just Topaz, I guess.

She said you felt bad for kicking me out of the gang.

If you think for one second that I feel bad for—

ROAR!

ROAR!!!

AAAAHHH!!!

ROAR!!!

Amethyst!!

Whoa!

Help!

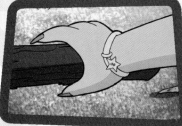

Don't worry, Am! I'm coming!

AAAAHHHH!!!

Hold on, Am!

Put her down!

67

Ow!

Don't worry, Am.
We're here.

Run!

Don't worry, Am. It's just Topaz.

Hey! I'll teach you to hurt my friend.

Uh, guys . . .

Nobody said anything about big sticks.

70

It's Topaz!

Topaz?

Well, duh! I mean, what other ogre would wear designer clothes?

So Amethyst was never in trouble?

We all know how much Amethyst means to you.

We just figured you needed a reminder.

Thanks for saving me from Topaz.

Don't get too pleased with yourself. I would have helped anybody.

Anybody?

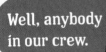 

Well, anybody in our crew.

Barf.

73

So it's okay that I changed over the summer?

You mean 'cause you grew up and stopped letting us push you around?

Yeah, I guess.

I was getting bored with the old Amethyst, anyway.

Are we all friends again?

Not just friends. BFFL!

Hey! Who's gonna change me back?

Best Friends For Life!

G'night!

See ya, Amethyst.

Don't let the bedbugs bite.

Topaz, how are you doing?

I think I ate a squirrel.

That is so gross.

Not to an ogre.

Next time Amethyst needs to be scared, *you* transform.

Look what I did to my shirt!

Okay, guys . . . let's hit the skoots.

Love ya!

Memory book on!

New photo.

That's better.

What a first day back!

I cast my first spell!!

But Ruby got jealous that I out-spelled her and kicked me out of the gang.

Then Onyx helped me understand that it wasn't my fault.

So she and Sapphire came up with some gelled magic . . .

. . . that turned Topaz into an ogre to scare Ruby . . .

. . . into remembering how much she cares about me.

Oh, no! What's left for tomorrow?

Congratrollations!

You get 50 Trollars to spend on Trollz.com just for buying this book!

After you've read the book go to Trollz.com and type in the code below to collect your 50 Trollars and have a chance to earn 300 more!

0-439-73386-386sv69c9ov64